KIDS CAN'T STOP READING
THE CHOOSE YOUR
OWN ADVENTURE® STORIES!

"Choose Your Own Adventure is the best thing that has come along since books themselves."
—Alysha Beyer, age 11

"I didn't read much before, but now I read my Choose Your Own Adventure books almost every night."
—Chris Brogan, age 13

"I love the control I have over what happens next."
—Kosta Efstathiou, age 17

"Choose Your Own Adventure books are so much fun to read and collect—I want them all!"
—Brendan Davin, age 11

And teachers like this series, too:
"We have read and reread, worn thin, loved, loaned, bought for others, and donated to school libraries our Choose Your Own Adventure books."

CHOOSE YOUR OWN ADVENTURE®—
AND MAKE READING MORE FUN!

CHOOSE YOUR OWN ADVENTURE®
titles in Large-Print Editions:

#66 SECRET OF THE NINJA
#88 MASTER OF KUNG FU
#92 RETURN OF THE NINJA
#97 THROUGH THE BLACK HOLE
#98 YOU ARE A MILLIONAIRE
#100 THE WORST DAY OF YOUR LIFE
#101 ALIEN, GO HOME!
#102 MASTER OF TAE KWAN DO
#106 HIJACKED!
#108 MASTER OF KARATE
#110 INVADERS FROM WITHIN
#112 SKATEBOARD CHAMPION
#114 DAREDEVIL PARK
#117 THE SEARCH FOR ALADDIN'S LAMP
#118 VAMPIRE INVADERS
#120 GHOST TRAIN
#121 BEHIND THE WHEEL
#122 MAGIC MASTER
#124 SUPERBIKE
#138 DINOSAUR ISLAND

All-Time Best-Sellers!

CHOOSE YOUR OWN ADVENTURE® • 97

THROUGH THE BLACK HOLE

BY EDWARD PACKARD

ILLUSTRATED BY FRANK BOLLE

Gareth Stevens Publishing
MILWAUKEE

For a free color catalog describing Gareth Stevens' list of high-quality
books, call 1-800-542-2595 (USA) or 1-800-461-9120 (Canada).
Gareth Stevens' Fax: (414) 225-0377.

Library of Congress Cataloging-in-Publication Data

Packard, Edward.
    Through the black hole/by Edward Packard; illustrated by
Frank Bolle.
       p. cm. — (Choose your own adventure; 97)
    Summary: The reader's decisions control the course of an adventure
in which two spaceships travel to investigate a black hole.
    ISBN 0-8368-1408-8
    1. Plot-your-own stories. [1. Black holes (Astronomy)—Fiction.
2. Science fiction. 3. Plot-your-own stories.] I. Bolle, Frank, ill.
II. Title. III. Series.
PZ7.P1245Tj   1995
[Fic]—dc20   95-21015

This edition first published in 1995 by
Gareth Stevens Publishing
1555 North RiverCenter Drive, Suite 201
Milwaukee, Wisconsin 53212 USA

CHOOSE YOUR OWN ADVENTURE® is a trademark of Bantam Doubleday Dell Books for
Young Readers, a division of Bantam Doubleday Dell Publishing Group, Inc.

Original conception of Edward Packard.
Interior illustrations by Frank Bolle. Cover art by Don Dixon.

Printed in the United States of America

1 2 3 4 5 6 7 8 9 99 98 97 96 95

THROUGH THE BLACK HOLE

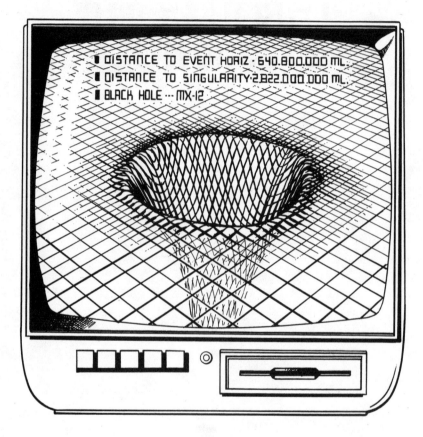

WARNING!!!

Do not read this book straight through from beginning to end. These pages contain many different adventures that you may have as you try to pilot your spacecraft toward a black hole. From time to time as you read along, you will be asked to make a choice. Your choice may lead to success or disaster!

The adventures you have are the results of your choices. You are responsible because you choose! After you make a choice, follow the instructions to see what happens to you next.

Think carefully before you make a decision. Once you leave the earth's gravity, anything can happen. Even if you are able to make it through the black hole to the other side, it doesn't necessarily mean that your mission has been a success!

Good luck!

You've never felt more excited. You've just graduated from the Space Academy, and you're waiting outside the office of Dr. Andre Bartok, the director of Interstellar Exploration. In a few moments you'll receive your first assignment in space.

You've hardly settled into your chair when a secretary calls, "Dr. Bartok will see you now."

The thin, balding director looks up from his computer terminal as you enter the room. "Come in—I've been expecting you." He smiles at you for a moment, then gestures for you to take a seat on the other side of his long, crescent-shaped desk.

You glance around the luxurious room. A huge montage of the Canopus star system lines one wall. Opposite it is a holographic display screen. Through the window behind the director's desk you can see the new *Athena* spaceship parked on the tarmac.

You hold your breath as you watch Dr. Bartok scanning your file for your assignment.

It seems like forever before he looks up from his screen. "You've had a brilliant record at the academy," he says. "Just about tops—and I want to send you on a mission of great importance. I'm going to give you a chance to pilot the *Athena*."

You practically fall out of your chair. Most of your experience has been in simulators and on training cruises—yet the *Athena* is the most advanced spaceship in the fleet. It has unbelievable speed and maneuvering capability.

Turn to page 2.

2

"Well," Dr. Bartok says, "are you interested?"

"Interested? I sure am. I can hardly believe it. I would have thought you'd want a much more experienced astronaut for such a mission."

"Of course I do," he says with a laugh. Then Dr. Bartok holds up his palm. His face becomes serious. "The reason you've been selected is *because* you're young. This mission requires a very long period of hibernation, and at least two major time dislocations. Our tests indicate that only someone around your age can withstand the stress involved. If we were to put you into this state of suspended animation when you were ten years older, you'd never wake up."

"I understand," you say after a moment. But you're beginning to feel a little nervous. "Just what is this mission about, Dr. Bartok? This isn't what I've heard rumors about—the first probe to the Pleiades star system?"

Dr. Bartok types a code into his computer. The room darkens slightly, and a projection of the Milky Way galaxy appears on the holographic screen. "We have in mind a much more important, more daring mission than that—nothing less than a trip to another universe. We want to send the *Athena* through MX-12, a black hole in the center of our galaxy."

Go on to the next page.

You sit dumbstruck, thinking of what you've learned about black holes at the academy. You know that a black hole is a place where matter is squeezed together—where gravity is so great that not even *light* can escape from it—which is why, if you were close enough to see it, it would look absolutely black. That in itself is frightening enough, but what's worse is that everything that enters a black hole keeps falling until it reaches a point where its entire mass, or weight, is compressed into nonexistence! Some scientists believe that all this mass can't completely disappear—that it has to go somewhere. They believe that in black holes there may be "wormholes" leading to another place and time. But it's scary to think of testing such a theory!

Turn to page 4.

4

"Good heavens, Dr. Bartok," you ask. "Would even the *Athena* have a chance to make it through a black hole? Wouldn't tidal forces rip any spaceship into neutrons before it reached the wormhole?"

Dr. Bartok glances at a document coming out of his fax machine. "That's the general rule," he says, "but the tidal forces diminish in proportion to the size of the black hole. If the black hole is rotating, and is big enough, it's theoretically possible to get through."

Those words *theoretically possible* bother you. No theory is really valid until it's been tested. And no human brain, or even the greatest computer, can be sure of what *really* goes on in a black hole. You're not eager to stake your life on some scientific theory.

Dr. Bartok must see the doubt in your face, because he says, "Of course, you don't have to go on this mission. I wouldn't have called you in except that on your questionnaire you said that you were ready for anything. There is another option. We're also going to send the *Athena*'s sister ship, the *Nimrod,* to the edge of the black hole. It will act as a backup and observer. Of course I must warn you, even going to the edge of a black hole is dangerous. And so, if you prefer, I'll be glad to assign you to the transport service."

Go on to the next page.

You don't particularly feel like risking your life, getting anywhere near a black hole. But to go into the transport service and spend the next ten years or so carrying rilium crystals back from Vega-9 or something like that isn't really much of an option.

"I'll accept the assignment, sir."

Dr. Bartok gets up and comes around to shake your hand. "I'm delighted," he says. "Now, do you choose to go on the observer ship, the *Nimrod,* or are you willing to go on the *Athena* itself and try to make it through the black hole?"

If you say you'll go on the Athena, *turn to page 14.*

If you say you'd rather go on the Nimrod, *turn to page 64.*

6

Cape Canaveral—three weeks later. Sixty seconds to takeoff. The *Athena* is in place on the launching pad. You and Nick Torrey, your copilot, are strapped into the command station. The onboard Mark VII celestial computer is functioning perfectly. It's programmed to guide the *Athena* to the very edge of MX-12: the massive black hole near the center of the galaxy.

The whole world is tuned to its video screens, watching as the countdown proceeds. Most people have praised your mission as being the most important space exploration in history, though some have said it's a waste of the government's money and could be a waste of your lives! Some of the top scientists in the world say you'll never get through—that no one, ever, can survive a trip through a black hole. For all you know, they may be right. You might not make it. But it's too late to change your mind now. A green light flashes on your instrument panel.

Nine, eight, seven, six, five, four, three, two, one . . .

BLAST OFF!

Turn to page 30.

8

When you wake, everything that has happened seems as if it were a dream—Baru-Kamm, the trip through the black hole, through the apple green space past the smooth gray planets, and then through the thick clay surface. Strangest of all is the memory of the inside-out world beneath the surface, with its fields of blue moss and multi-colored plants, its upside-down mountains and violet-hued oceans in the sky. . . .

You glance over at Nick. There's a dazed look on his face.

"Nick, when did you wake up?"

"Just a few minutes ago," he says. "I've been trying to figure out whether we went through the black hole or whether I just dreamed it."

"I think we went through it," you say. "Unless we were both dreaming."

"I can't get over it," Nick says. "It was so weird."

"It sure was," you say. "But right now I'm worried about getting home."

You're relieved that you recognize some familiar constellations. You quickly take bearings on a few stars and punch the data into the computer.

A few seconds later you point to the display screen. "Nick, the computer says we're only forty light years from Earth."

"That's not much help," he says. "Look at the number three monitor. We're completely out of fuel!"

Turn to page 61.

You stare out of first one view port and then another. Everywhere you look is the same vaporous apple green color, except for directly behind the ship, where you can make out a small whitish patch in the sky.

"Is that where we came from?" you ask Nick.

"No doubt," he says. "I've been keeping an eye on it since I woke up. It's getting smaller by the minute."

"So on this side, the black hole is white!"

"We've learned that much, at least," says Nick. "And that space in this universe must be filled with some kind of gas; otherwise it would look black, the way it does in our universe."

"But if it were filled with gas, then we'd be slowing down and heating up, the way we do when we enter a planet's atmosphere."

Nick looks at you for a moment. "You're right." He punches some keys on the computer. In a moment he reports. "Not surprising, I guess. Our sensors can't account for the green glow around us."

"I guess it's caused by yet another law that's different from ours," you say.

"We may never find out what those laws are," Nick says. "Our sensors show nothing at all, except that we're traveling at infinite speed."

"Let's see if the ship can still maneuver." You instruct the computer to first increase and then decrease power, then to turn at various angles. Everything works, but very sluggishly. Time seems to be moving at a slower rate than in your own universe.

Turn to page 65.

10

Suddenly you have hope: a round, grayish shape—what seems to be a planet—is growing larger in the sky as you approach it. Soon you see dozens of them. They come in many different sizes, but each one looks as smooth as a billiard ball.

"They don't look as if they would support human life," Nick says.

"No, they don't, but let's get as close a look at one as we can."

The *Athena* speeds by several of the smooth gray planets; you see one that appears to be about the size of the earth.

"Let's head for that one," you say.

Nick gives a thumbs-up. "I'm swinging her now," he says. "I'll put the braking thrusters on standby—we don't know how strong gravity will be on this planet."

"Good thinking," you say. But soon you see that gravity isn't going to be a problem. Your rate of approach keeps slowing, even as you apply more power!

Turn to page 69.

12

Suddenly Nick's face loses its color. A red light is flashing on the control monitor. It's a major malfunction!

Nick stares at you. "Why did this have to happen now?" He's punching in a detailed data request.

Your eyes are fixed on the monitor. "It's this terrific gravitational field we're in. Come on, computer, we need information!"

The computer replies fast enough, but you don't feel any happier when you read the words on the screen.

Starboard thruster crack: condition progressive; requires emergency EV repair, procedure: 42–553. Probable time to irreversibility 88 seconds, 87, 86, 85 . . .

You and Nick don't have to discuss what this means—you've been trained for almost any emergency. "EV repair" means someone will have to go outside the spaceship and repair the damage. "Condition progressive" means that the crack is getting worse every second. If the computer is right, it's going to split wide open in a little over a minute!

Go on to the next page.

"Will you do it, or shall I?" Nick asks.

The answer doesn't depend on how brave you are—it depends on who can fix the crack faster. You're more athletic than Nick. You're sure you could get in position faster; on the other hand, he has a knack with mechanical things that you don't. That might make the difference.

If you try to make the repair yourself, turn to page 18.

If you tell Nick to make the repair, turn to page 68.

14

"I'll take my chances on the *Athena,*" you answer.

Dr. Bartok nods vigorously. "Excellent—I wish I could go myself. If you make it, you'll view things that could never be seen on Earth, or even in our galaxy—things that are literally out of this universe!"

"Who will be my copilot, sir?"

"Nick Torrey."

What a break—Nick is one of your best friends! "I'm very excited," you say.

You don't mention it, but you're also scared. If things don't go well, you'll end up as a few trillion neutrons scattered by the massive forces of the black hole.

Turn to page 6.

"Let's turn back the other way," Nick says. "At least then we'll be pointed in the direction we're moving."

It takes another hour to bring the ship back on its original course. By this time the fuzzy white patch is completely out of sight.

Nick sighs. "I guess we're stuck in this universe." His voice breaks as he says this.

"Worse than that," you say. "We're going to starve, if we don't run out of oxygen."

"Hey, look at that!" Nick points ahead, a little to the right of the ship.

Turn to page 10.

"Let's take our chances," you say. "It looks real interesting on the other side."

Nick walks up to the river's edge and stares at the flowing waters. "Yeah, *if* we make it to the other side. . . ."

You pick up a stick, toss it into midstream, and watch it float with the current. "Why shouldn't we make it across?" you say. "The river's not very deep, and look at that stick. We could swim faster than that current if we really had to."

"Okay," Nick says. "Let's try it, but you first."

You start wading cautiously across the river. Nick follows a few steps behind. Even when you reach the middle, it's only up to your hips. The current is flowing at its fastest here, but you don't feel in any danger of being swept off your feet.

You take a few more steps. Already the water is getting shallower! You half turn and look back. "Come on, Nick—I'm almost—"

You never finish your sentence. Something has seized your leg in a viselike grip. You look down and realize why you didn't see it sooner. It's a creature very much like a crocodile except that it's pink, the same color pink as the bottom of the river!

"Nick, get back!" you scream—then you're pulled under the swirling waters.

The End

18

"I'll make the repair, Nick." You snap on your space helmet, grab a tool kit, and step inside the air lock. A second later a buzzer tells you it's safe to proceed. You open the outer hatch, snap on your tether, and swing out into space. Your legs float straight out as you grab the EV rail and move hand over hand toward the starboard thruster.

The scene around you is frightening. A huge part of the sky ahead of the ship is the coal black disk that's growing larger every second.

The computer is patched into the radio in your helmet. You can hear the seconds remaining ticking off: *47, 46, 45* . . . It will take almost that long just to reach the thruster, and at least ten seconds to laser seal the crack. It's going to be tight.

Suddenly you remember the jet pack on your space suit. If you could give just the right burst of power, you could get to the thruster in only a few seconds. Of course, if you use too much power you'll overshoot.

If you try to get a burst of speed with your jet pack, turn to page 102.

If you keep working your way hand over hand, turn to page 56.

You set course for the other ship at maximum speed. "How close to the black hole can we get?" you ask Nick.

He's already punching data into the computer; then the question: "What are our chances of rescuing the crew of the *Athena?*"

The answer comes back at once.

Chance of rescuing Athena *crew and escaping black hole: 22%.*

Chance of not succeeding in rescuing Athena *crew but escaping black hole: 18%.*

Chance of being swept into black hole along with Athena *crew: 41%.*

Variability factor—no prediction possible: 19%.

"There you have it," Nick says. "What shall we do?"

If you try to rescue the Athena *crew, turn to page 53.*

If you decide it's too risky, turn to page 63.

20

Nick walks up close to Baru. "Are you an android?" he asks as the two of you sit down.

Baru laughs "No, we are not an android any more than we are a god or a magician. An android is programmed by its builder and can only do what it is programmed to do. The body we are in is like that of an android, but that is only a temporary convenience. We can place our mind anywhere— in a swarm of butterflies, or in anything we want."

"There are many things we don't understand about this universe," Nick says. "Out in space it seemed to us that gravity repelled instead of attracted. But somehow it's holding us here on the ground—we feel almost as heavy here as we do on Earth."

"It is not gravity that holds you to the ground," Baru says. "It's the antigravity of the white star in the center of this planet."

"What do you mean?" you say, looking up overhead. "I don't see a star."

Go on to the next page.

"You can't see it," Baru says, "because it's only a few feet across. It's a tiny white hole in the cosmos. It is the repulsive force of the tiny white hole that hollowed out this planet. This same force keeps you from rising up in the air. And the star's energy provides the light by which we see— though this spreads so evenly through the air that it doesn't seem to be coming from any one point."

"This is hard to understand," Nick says.

Baru smiles. "Only because it's the opposite of what you're used to. If you had been born here and visited Earth, you would find it most peculiar to be living on the outside surface of a planet. You would probably grab hold of a tree to keep from flying off into space."

Turn to page 104.

22

Slowly you become conscious. You're alive—and you're on another spaceship! A familiar figure is standing over your bunk. It's Jack Willard—you knew him at the academy!

"Jack—am I dreaming?"

"You're not," he says, smiling down on you. "You're on the *Liberty.* Command decided we should follow you as an extra backup. We were lucky to reach you in time."

"How's Nick?"

"He's fine," Willard says. "No sign of the *Nimrod,* though."

"They're lost, Jack," you say. "We picked up their beamer. They had a power failure and were sucked into the black hole."

He shakes his head. "We were afraid that might have happened." After a while he says, "I guess you'll be mighty glad to get back to Earth."

"I sure will," you say. "But I'm not through trying. Someday I'm going to make it through the black hole."

The End

24

Why would the hatch be jammed? you wonder. Maybe it's because of relativistic effects. At this incredible speed they're getting more extreme every second!

You can't leave Nick outside the spaceship while you're entering a black hole. You've got to get the hatch open, and fast! You run to it and activate the electronic controls. Nothing. You try the emergency levers. They won't move. The metal is bent. You race back to the computer and type in: *"Hatch inoperable. Metal expanded by effects near black hole. What is the best action possible?"*

You wait for the computer to respond. You're not even sure it's programmed for the solution to the problem. Precious seconds are ticking away.

At last a response comes up on the screen:

Apply minimum of 600 pounds pressure evenly to exterior of hatch surface.

Good grief! That's no help. There's no way Nick could apply such pressure!

Desperately you type in: *"What is the best way to apply pressure?"*

You have to wait almost ten more seconds for the two-word reply:

Centrifugal force.

Go on to the next page.

You almost scream with frustration. Why is the computer being so slow and so unhelpful? Then you remember that it is the best on-board computer ever built. No other computer its size could handle such a range of problems. But you don't have time to ask it more questions. You've got to use the computer in your brain!

You know that you could use centrifugal force to open the hatch. All you have to do is adjust your course slightly.

You only have to decide which direction to turn the ship to cause the hatch to swing inward. The door is on the starboard, or right, side of the ship. Should you turn the *Athena* slightly to starboard, or should you turn it left to port?

*If you adjust course to starboard,
turn to page 38.*

If you adjust course to port, turn to page 46.

26

You pull out your laser pistol and aim it at the latch. Slowly you squeeze the trigger. A burst of light streaks out, but it's following a curve—the laser light is bent in an arc! Instead of reaching the hatch, it curves back toward the stern of the ship, where the liquid hydrogen is stored. How could that happen? Suddenly you realize why: you're traveling at nearly the speed of light in a massive gravitational field. Of course the light ray would be bent!

This thought has hardly crossed your mind when the liquid hydrogen explodes in a weirdly distorted flare of light. The blast tears the *Athena*, Nick, and you into bits of matter that are soon reduced to neutrons, then disappear completely as they reach the center of the black hole.

The End

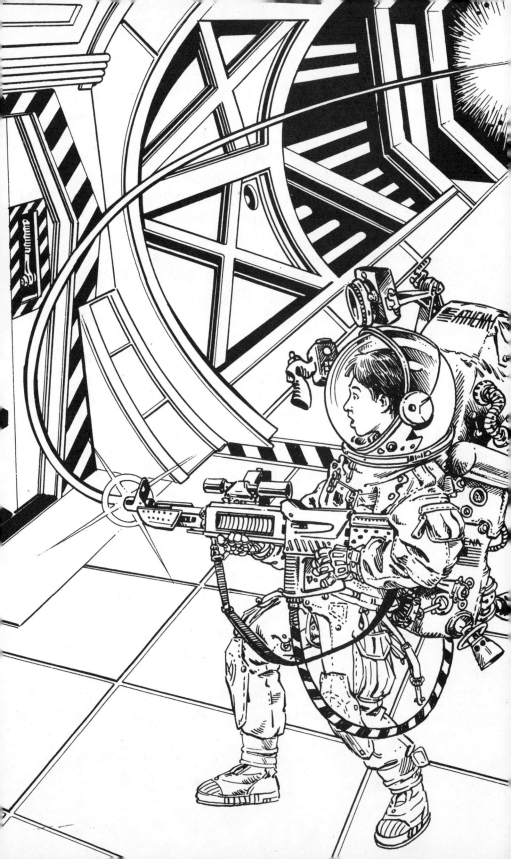

28

Suddenly your mission has changed. Instead of being the observers, you and Nick are the ones who must try to make it through the black hole! The only trouble is that you haven't been maneuvering in the precise way necessary to gain entrance to the wormhole. The ship is already creaking and groaning from the gravitational differential between the bow and the stern. Even your own body is being stretched. Gravity now is so intense that the part of you nearest the black hole is falling faster than the part of your body farthest from it!

You hear Nick's voice, croaking, as if even his vocal chords are being stretched toward the breaking point. "I've put the computer on autopilot and told it to get us into the wormhole. All we can do is hope."

You're pinned against your restraints as the computer adjusts course and speed. The scene outside the view port is indescribably weird. Behind you is nothing but a faint red glow. Ahead, space is completely black, except for a ghostly halo of dark violet and purple. In the center of the halo is the singularity, the source of the terrifying gravitational field that is pulling you in, and which is probably about to crush you. Your only hope is that some unknown force is at work in this strange place, a force that can lead you into another universe!

Your fingers are shaking as you punch a question into the computer: "Can you steer us into the wormhole?"

Turn to page 75.

A second later all is calm again, and your dizziness passes. You send the radio signal that should cause the hatch to open. Nothing happens. You try again. Still nothing. Vibrations must have knocked the micro locks out of alignment—you'll have to open it by hand.

"What's the matter?" Nick yells in your headphone. "Are you having—"

His voice cuts out.

"Nick?"

No reply. You wonder what happened.

You struggle with a spanner wrench, trying to loosen the hatch. Your hands are shaking. You feel drained of energy. Suddenly the hatch opens. A heavy object strikes your shoulder. You stare, horrified, as you see the door whirling off into space! You can get into the air lock now, but there's no way you'll be able to get back inside the cabin— the inside door is designed not to open unless the outer door is closed. Of course, you could blast it open, but then the cabin would be depressurized, all the oxygen would escape, and everything loose would be sucked out into space.

You shout in your mike. "Nick, Nick, can you hear me?"

There is no answer.

You're trapped in space with only a few hours of oxygen left, and you can't even talk to Nick! You look helplessly around you, and at that moment the whole sky goes black.

Turn to page 106.

30

You are in deep space aboard the *Athena*. You and Nick have awakened from a hibernation of several years. Following its instructions, the computer did not stir you until the *Athena* was a few hundred billion light years from the black hole. You're close enough now so that you've both donned your space suits to be ready for any emergency. You and Nick have just made final course adjustments. With the computer's help, you plan to ride a gravity wave into a wormhole that you hope will lead to another universe. You just hope the calculations are right. The slightest error in speed and course will mean certain death.

The view through the windows is awesome. You're traveling so fast that the whole sky is distorted by relativistic effects. Most of the stars and nebulae seem clustered behind you. They've all taken on an eerie, reddish-orange glow. The stars ahead of you, on the other hand, have a purplish violet hue. In the center of them is a coal black disk—the black hole itself.

"It's so eerie," Nick says to you softly. "That black disk is expanding even as we look at it—taking up more and more of the sky."

"One thing it took me a while to understand," you say, "is that even when we're surrounded by blackness, we won't actually be in the wormhole."

"No," Nick says. "We'll be just inside the event horizon—within the sphere from which no light escapes."

A buzzer sounds.

Turn to page 12.

You and Nick stare at each other in disbelief. You can't tell where the voice is coming from—it's as if you are surrounded by hi-fi speakers.

"Who are you? Where are you?" you shout into the air. The answer comes back instantly.

"We are the mind of Baru-Kamm."

"What does that mean?" Nick asks.

There is no answer, and at that moment the butterflies flutter away, like a vanishing multicolored cloud.

Nick points after them. "*That* was the mind of Baru-Kamm!"

Turn to page 92.

32

Nick has a mournful expression on his face. "It looks as if we're stuck here," he says.

Baru holds up one hand. "There is one chance," Baru says. "Just as we can reorganize our atoms and subatoms into those of a humanlike person or a swarm of butterflies, we could organize your atoms into another shape."

"But we'd still be repelled, too, wouldn't we?" Nick asks.

Baru smiles. "Not if the mind of Baru-Kamm transformed you into *negative* particles. Instead of being repelled, they would be drawn into the white hole and then emerge as positive particles in your own universe. They would then transform into their original state—meaning *you.*"

"That's far beyond any science we have on Earth," Nick says, "but after what I've seen here, I'm willing to believe you can do it."

"But even if you could," you say, "and we were able to emerge again in our own universe, wouldn't we find ourselves just floating through space?"

"No," says Baru. "Because we would transmit not only you, but your own spaceship!"

"We'd still have a tough time finding our way back home," you say. "Besides, our ship is almost out of fuel."

Go on to the next page.

"You will learn," says Baru, "that you will be able to do much that you could not do before."

"What do you mean?"

The strange alien fastens a hypnotic gaze upon you. "We shall impart you with the mind of Baru-Kamm."

These ideas make you dizzy. And judging by the way Nick looks, they must make him even dizzier. "What shall we do?" he asks you.

If you decide to try to go through the white hole, turn to page 112.

If you decide to stay where you are, turn to page 70.

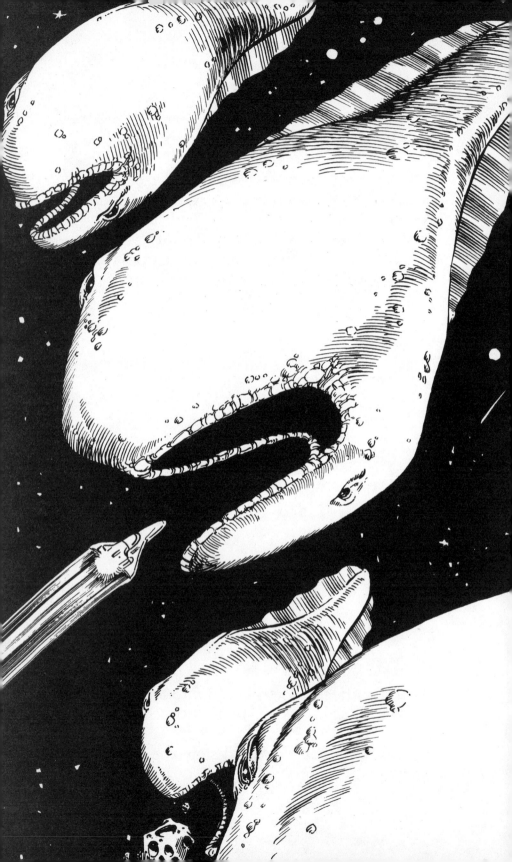

You continue to cruise through the apple green space. You pass stray planets and asteroids, a couple of dwarf stars, and other debris, but not a single livable planet. You're feeling pretty discouraged when Nick almost jumps out of his seat.

"Over there!" Nick points out the starboard view port at a huge object. It looks like a gigantic flying mitten! It must be a thousand miles long, or even more, and it keeps opening and closing a mouth that seems to take up half its length.

"There's another one of them," you say, "and there's more behind them."

Suddenly the leading object changes course. With incredible speed it snaps up an asteroid, and then a small comet.

"They're alive!" Nick says.

You watch a few seconds more. "I think you're right. They're scavengers—feeding on debris spouting out of the white hole!"

"They may want to feed on us," Nick says. "Let's get out of here!"

You glance out the other view port. One of the creatures is coming straight at you!

"Full power!" you scream at Nick.

The *Athena* accelerates—like a little fish swimming into the jaws of a whale.

The End

36

"It's more important for us to find water," you say.

"It's a long way up there to that water." Nick points upward, to where the sky would be if you were on Earth. But because you are standing on the planet's inner surface, he's pointing not at the sky, but at the other side of the world.

"Nick," you say, "we don't even know if that is water, or even if water exists in this universe. We haven't seen a cloud in the sky."

"Yet it doesn't feel dry. It's got to rain here," Nick says, "or there wouldn't be plants."

"Maybe it only rains at night," you say.

Nick looks at you strangely. "Come to think of it, I have a funny feeling it's always daytime here."

Suddenly a horde of brilliantly colored butterflies flutters by. Their colors are so beautiful that they seem to give off their own light!

You and Nick stare in wonder at them as they hover, like tiny helicopters. Then a clear, musical voice fills the air.

"You shall find water in the hollows of purple vines, like the ones beyond the ridge. You may eat plants or berries that are orange, red, or yellow, but do not eat anything else. Always watch out for the green bears. Sleep and rest only in beds of lavender moss. The bears do not like its aroma and will not attack you there. Do not cross the river that flows over pink sand. Remember these things and you shall live happily on Baru-Kamm."

Turn to page 31.

An eternity seems to pass—though it may only be days, or hours, or seconds, you'll never know. And nothing has changed, except that you have slowly become aware that you are in total darkness. The lights in your spaceship have either gone out, or you have gone blind. There's no way of telling because you still can't move.

If you could only report back to Earth what has happened. It would be of great interest to scientists to learn that a spaceship sent into a massive black hole will not necessarily be torn apart or crushed, that it may become simply suspended in time. But of course you'll never be able to tell anyone. Even if you could move enough to work the radio, no signal could escape from within the black hole.

If only you could talk to Nick. Perhaps you can reach him through mental telepathy. *Nick . . . Nick . . . can you hear my thoughts?* But it's no use. The harder you try, the more your mind fuzzes over.

For a moment you think that you might sleep, but you're unable to do even that. You can only sit motionless, waiting for that which can never come.

Turn to page 58.

38

Acting to adjust course to starboard, you command the computer to fire a minimal burst from the port thruster. Instantly the *Athena* turns very slightly to the right. At this speed, even this extremely slight course change produces an inertial force of over six Gs. You're thrown inward, hard against your restraints. The inertial force has opened the hatch! Nick flies in, landing on his feet on the side of the hull opposite the hatch. Fortunately his heavy space boots absorb the shock. A moment later the air in the cabin rushes out through the open hatch. Nick goes floating wildly around the cabin, coming to rest only when he's able to grab the handholds near the air lock.

You hear his voice in the radio on your helmet. "Thanks for getting me in here. I'll get this hatch shut so we can repressurize."

"Okay," you answer as you adjust the ship back on course. "Let me know if you can use some help." But even as you're speaking, you can see that no help will be enough. The force was so strong it not only forced the hatch open, it ripped it from its hinges!

Nick kicks off a wall and floats over to his control station a few feet away from yours. Neither of you says anything. It's obvious you're in deep trouble—headed directly for a black hole, with the hatch door open, trapped in your space suits with a limited supply of air.

It's dangerous enough trying to get through a black hole under perfect conditions. To continue on now would be suicide.

Turn to page 84.

40

Nick's jaw is hanging open. "You're some kind of god," he says.

"Or a magician," you add.

Baru smiles. "No, we are neither a god or a magician. Everything you see, we have achieved by science."

You step in and gaze closely at the alien who looks so much like a human being. "But how . . . how do you know we're from Earth—how can you speak our language?"

"We scanned your computer's memory—it contains the complete record of your flight and much information about you and your home planet."

"You dug through the tunnel to our spaceship?"

"There was no need to dig," Baru replies. "We are able to scan everything electronically." The alien sits on a patch of lavender moss and crosses its legs. "In this body we find it more comfortable to sit rather than stand. You may sit, too, if you like."

Turn to page 20.

You quickly instruct the computer to reverse course and seek out the *Nimrod.*

"Make sure you're locked tightly in your restraints," you tell Nick as you punch instructions into the computer. "We have no time to waste."

You knew you were pretty close to the point of no return. Still, you're not prepared for the pressure as the computer orders maximum power to bring the *Athena* on its new course. Though the event horizon of the black hole is still hundreds of millions of miles away, the gravitational force here is incredibly great. Only a supremely advanced space drive like the *Athena*'s could break such a grip.

The ship turns ever so slowly, following an arc through space tens of millions of miles long. At the crest of the arc—the point where you're closest to the black hole and the gravitational force is the strongest—the ship seems to hover, as if it can't decide which force to yield to. You bite your lip. Beads of sweat are falling down your face. The view plate of your helmet fogs up. The slightest loss of power now would mean certain destruction. The seconds tick by. Slowly at first, then more quickly, the distance to the black hole begins to lengthen.

You hear Nick's voice in your speaker. "It's too soon to celebrate, but I think we're going to make it."

You give him the thumbs-up sign.

Turn to page 89.

You punch number 2.

Scientists on Earth have thought up many theories about what it would be like in a massive black hole. Most of them say that you would be torn apart by a gravity field millions of times stronger than that on Earth. But some say that if the black hole were rotating, and you entered at just the right speed and just the right angle, the centrifugal force would balance the gravitational force as you entered the hole and you might safely pass through.

Sometimes such theories are right, sometimes wrong, and sometimes they are half right and half wrong. You are now about to find out, as the *Nimrod* plunges at almost the speed of light toward the singularity—the terrible vortex.

One thing soon becomes clear and gives you hope. This hole you're falling into *is* rotating, and the centrifugal force that has been set up almost precisely balances the force of gravity. Gradually, the *Nimrod* begins to whirl around the vortex, like a speck in a column of water swirling around and around on its way down a drain. Turbulence might jostle a speck away from the wall of water, causing it to fall straight down.

But this does not happen to the *Nimrod*. Instead, it whirls around and around the black hole for thousands, and hundreds of thousands, and millions of years. In some future eon, your skeleton, and Nick's, will finally pass through the black hole.

The End

44

You cruise toward home, but with the hatch cover missing, and the cabin depressurized, there's no way of going into hibernation. Your oxygen supply can't last more than a few weeks—enough to travel no more than a few billion miles. There are thousands of earth ships traveling in space, but the chances of one of them sighting you must be about one in a million.

The days pass. You're traveling at tremendous speed, but the stars ahead of you don't seem to get any closer. You and Nick rarely say anything to each other. It would use up too much energy, too much oxygen.

Finally it comes—the low, repeating beep that means you have only three more hours of oxygen left in your space suit. There's nothing to do now but wait for the end.

It's not long before your head begins to ache. You feel increasingly dizzy. Your brain goes numb from lack of oxygen. Then you pass out.

Turn to page 22.

You set course for the planet Nicron. The computer reports that it's only twenty-three billion miles away. You should be able to get there in a few days.

"Search the data file," Nick says. "I know a probe was received from there some years ago."

You're already asking the computer to scan its memory. "Yeah, we have quite a bit of information about Nicron," you say. "As I remember, it's quite similar to the Earth. It has a moon and is at just the right distance from its sun."

"Sounds good," Nick says. "Someone told me that it was almost a perfect planet, with plenty of food and resources, beautiful forests and lakes, everything we could want!"

"Yeah, I heard that, too," you say. "But for some reason it's not a good place to live."

"I wonder why?" Nick says.

A moment later the answer comes up on the screen.

Planet Nicron: Analysis: Nicron is a perfect planet. It has every resource to be found on Earth and no pollution. However, all spaceships are advised to stay away from it. Nicron and its sun and moon are all falling toward the black hole—they will reach it in seven months, three days, six hours, and two minutes.

The End

46

Acting to adjust course to port, you command the computer to fire a minimal burst from the starboard thruster. This causes the ship to turn slightly to the left. At this speed, even a very slight course change produces an inertial force of over six Gs! You're thrown hard against your restraints—and it hurts. But what hurts more is realizing that you've been thrown to the right instead of the left. The hatch has not only opened, it has flown off into space and taken poor Nick with it!

The G forces subside—the *Athena* is traveling in a straight line now—but you feel horrible. You must have been suffering from space fatigue to make such a mistake. Poor Nick. And poor you! The course change you just made put the *Athena* on the wrong angle of approach to the black hole! There's almost no chance of avoiding destruction now. You quickly instruct the computer to compensate for the variation, but you're too late—you can already feel the controls shuddering, the cracks opening in the hull, and then nothing, as the *Athena* is crushed in the singularity.

The End

"Well," Nick says, "we'll just have to hope the computer is wrong. Maybe we should start for home and hope that another spaceship is cruising way out here."

"I guess so, unless we want to hope for another miracle and try to make it through the black hole."

"Either way it seems hopeless," Nick says.

You shrug. You have to agree with him, and, as if you weren't having enough trouble, your space suit isn't working right. It feels like a steam bath inside.

If you try to cruise toward home for as long as you can, turn to page 44.

If you try to head the Athena back toward the black hole, turn to page 86.

"Let's think a moment," you say. "If we tried to back out of here, we'd have to start from a dead stop. We'd be almost sure to get stuck in the clay."

"I wonder how far we are from the inner surface?" Nick asks.

"Wait a second." You ask the computer for a density analysis of the clay ahead of the ship. A few seconds later it reports: *Infinite density.*

Nick laughs. "That's its way of saying it can't figure things out in this universe," he says. "Let's try an ultrasonic probe."

"Good thinking."

It takes a moment for the UP screen to light up. You position the pointer, touch a button, and send an ultrasonic beam shooting out ahead of the ship. You and Nick watch the squiggly waves that appear on the monitor. Just as you'd hoped, the pattern of sound waves changes once they reach the inner surface of the planet. In a moment a digital reading appears: *Distance to discontinuity: 3.7 meters.*

"We're almost there!" Nick shouts.

"What luck!" You run over to shake his hand. The inner surface is hardly more than ten yards away!

Go on to the next page.

Nick's smile fades. "We're still going to have to tunnel through that stuff."

"We can do it," you say. "We can cut a tunnel that far with the jets on our space suits."

Nick has a blank look on his face. You know he must be calculating something in his head. "We should be able to make it," he says. "Judging by how thick the clay is, I think it would take about an hour."

"We can carry enough oxygen for that," you say.

"I guess so," Nick says. "It looks like we'll reach the inner surface. But what then? There's not much chance we'll be able to stay alive once we're there."

"Maybe not," you say. "But there wasn't much chance we'd get this far—and yet we did. So let's get started!"

Turn to page 91.

"We can't just leave them, Nick—let's go for it."

"Right on," he says.

You're already punching instructions into the computer. In less than a minute, the *Nimrod* is speeding toward its sister ship. You radio the crew of the *Athena* that you're coming, though you're almost certain the message won't go through. The magnetic force field here breaks up radio waves.

You're straining the space drive to the maximum, trying to reach the other ship before both of you slip below the event horizon—the point of no return.

You ask the computer for the latest probability profile and gasp when the words appear on the screen:

Chance of rescuing the Athena: 0.

"Nick, look at the screen!"

His face is ashen. "But . . . why?"

You're already asking the computer the same question. In a moment the answer appears:

Athena destroyed by tidal forces of rotating black hole.

You have failed to rescue the crew of the *Athena,* and you're in peril yourself! You command the computer to execute escape maneuvers. Instead you get another horrifying message.

Passing through the event horizon.

"There's no way back now," Nick says.

Turn to page 28.

54

Your ship is still coasting, but it's rapidly slowing down.

Nick looks frightened. He says the same words that are in your mind. "We may be trapped here forever."

At that moment your ship comes to a dead halt. You and Nick sit and look at each other.

"I would rather have floated forever in space," you say. "Though I suppose it doesn't really make any difference."

"There's only one hope," Nick says. "The computer reports that our reverse thrusters aren't jammed. If they still work, we might be able to back out the way we came in."

"If we're going to do that, we better try soon," you say. "The longer we wait, the more likely the clay will seep into those valves, too."

"Well," says Nick. "Shall we try it then?"

If you attempt to back out of the planet, turn to page 77.

If you decide to take the time to consider other options, turn to page 50.

You're desperate, but you can't see anything to be gained by blasting open the door. What's more, if Nick is still alive, he'll lose all his oxygen and could be hurt by depressurization. It's not worth risking both your lives.

But what else can you do? By now you must be traveling very close to the speed of light. Within minutes you may reach the singularity, where all matter falling into the black hole is compressed into a geometrical point. How this can happen is a paradox—a situation that seems impossible but isn't.

Turn to page 96.

56

You work your way along, hand over hand, across the side of the ship. You're weightless and able to move easily. In a few seconds you reach the thruster. You locate the crack with the X-ray sensor fitted to your helmet, then punch the coordinates into your laser welder and apply it along the fault line. An electronic tone in your sensor tells you when the crack is filled. At the same time the relay from the on-board computer stops its countdown. Condition restored to normal. The whole operation took eight seconds. You did it with eleven seconds to spare!

You're feeing pretty good as you work your way back toward the outer hatch. You take a moment to look around. The part of the sky where the ship is headed is a vast black disk. Surrounding this disk, and extending the full 180 degrees behind you, is a shimmering ring of deep red light.

You hear Nick's voice in your earphones.

"You did a great job, pal, but get back in here. We're coming up fast on the event horizon—traveling at 90 percent of light speed!"

You feel rather dizzy as you work your way back toward the hatch. Suddenly you're quivering. The whole ship is vibrating. You're crossing the event horizon—the edge of the whirlpool—the point from which nothing, not even light, can return.

Turn to page 29.

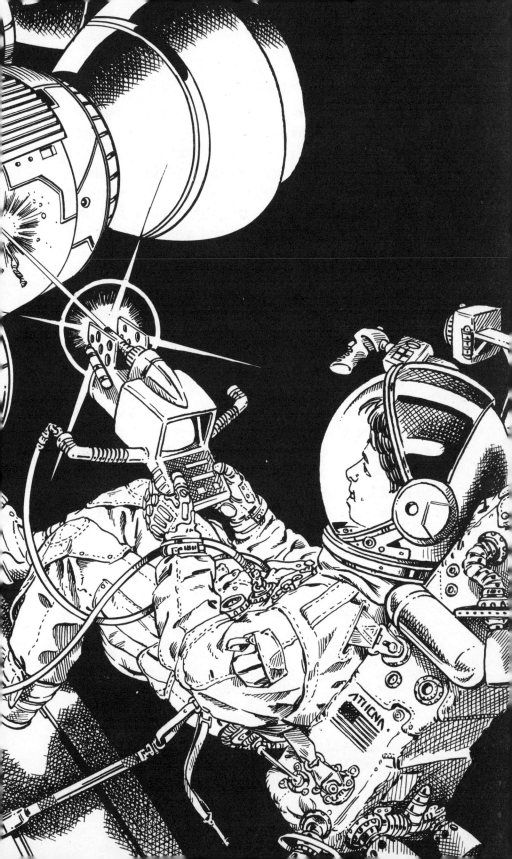

58

You're not sure how much time has passed. At first you think you're back home in your own bed, then you think you're in the hospital. But it's not a doctor standing by your bunk, it's Nick smiling down at you.

"I'm glad you came out of it, pal—I've only been awake a few minutes, but I was already feeling pretty lonely."

You sit up and look around, rubbing your eyes. Only then do you remember that you're inside a spaceship, and that before you became unconscious you were falling into a black hole. You look through the view port. The sky isn't black; instead, it's a sort of pleasing apple green.

"Nick, did we make it?"

He nods. "We're on the other side." His voice is really soft, as if the two of you had entered a tomb, or a great cathedral. You know he feels the way you do—filled with awe. There's something about the light that makes you feel different, as if you're in a place beyond space and time. And that, of course, is what's happened. You have entered another universe.

You glance at the status screen. It reads:
Course: undeterminable
Speed: infinity

Go on to the next page.

"Nick, I don't care if *we have* entered another universe—we can't be traveling at infinite speed."

"I don't think *we are*," he says, "but *we* may be traveling at faster than what light speed is in our own universe. The computer would register that as infinity."

"So the laws of physics *are* different here," you say.

"Some of them must be," Nick says. "That could help us, or it could hurt us."

Turn to page 9.

60

You punch number 1.

The black hole is rotating, and as you plunge toward the singularity, centrifugal force almost precisely matches the gravitational force. As a result, you are not torn apart by gravity. Instead, you float weightlessly as the *Nimrod* whirls around and around the vortex of the hole.

The forces here are so great that even the mighty thrusters of the *Nimrod* have no effect. Your only hope is that a quantum fluctuation—some unpredictable disturbance—will save you. Normally, the chances of such a thing happening are one in trillions. But the rules are different inside a black hole. The forces are so great that the laws of physics are altered in ways that could never be tested on Earth. As it happens, a quantum disturbance flicks the *Nimrod* out of the whirlpool. Suddenly it's plunging straight into the singularity!

Exactly what happens then you'll never know—the forces are so great that you lose consciousness. Nor would scientists be able to explain—the laws of physics here are different from anything observed on Earth. But when you come to, you know that you must have passed safely to the other side—for things are very different than they were.

Turn to page 111.

"We'll have to think of how to convert part of the ship into energy," you say.

Nick looks at you strangely. "Yes, I'm sure we can do that."

You feel sure of it, too.

You stand up and stretch your arms and legs. It will be good to be back on Earth again and see your family and friends. You go back to the bathroom and look in the mirror. You look well rested—very strong and healthy, in fact. But there's something a little different about your face. It looks smoother, almost better formed than you remember. You recognize yourself—there's no doubt about that—and yet you are no longer *just* you—you are *more* than you. It's too soon to tell what that means exactly. But it will mean many things for the future, of that you are sure—within your mind is the mind of Baru-Kamm.

The End

"The odds are just too much against us," you tell Nick. "I can't see how we could rescue them without risking our own lives. We'd probably be sucked into the black hole after them. I think we'll have to return to the base."

You start punching in the coordinates for the return flight to Earth. "At least we'll have gathered new data on black holes," you say.

As the booster thrusters fire, and the *Nimrod* swings onto its new course, your eyes remain fixed on the deep reddish glow that surrounds the black hole. You can't get your mind off the astronauts who may already have been crushed into oblivion. You glance at Nick. He, too, seems hypnotized by the sight. And so neither you nor Nick are looking at the display screen of the area ahead of you. It's not until an audio warning sounds that you're aware of the stray comet hurtling across your path on its way into the black hole. Normally you would still have plenty of time to alter your course. But the tremendous gravity of the black hole has accelerated the comet to almost a tenth of the speed of light. By the time you become aware of it, it's over ten thousand miles away, but your hand hasn't even reached the evasion switch when it strikes.

The End

64

You have just awoken from hibernation. Several years have passed since you accepted your mission. You're aboard the spaceship *Nimrod,* as commander. Your mission is to observe your sister ship, the *Athena,* as it attempts to pass through the black hole. You and your crew mate, Nick Torrey, are trying to stay as close to the *Athena* as possible in case of any trouble. On the other hand, you don't want to get *too* close or you'll be sucked into the hole yourself.

The stars behind you appear as reddish, glowing clusters because of the effects of relativity. You're now traveling almost as fast as the *Athena,* but you're having difficulty staying in contact with her because of the enormous magnetic forces surrounding the black hole. For a while you're completely out of communication. Then a faint message comes through—a call for help: the *Athena's* main engines have failed!

Turn to page 19.

"At some point we may want to get back home," Nick says. "Let's turn around and head toward the black hole—I mean the white hole. I want to see if we can get closer to it."

You feel the same way. In a second or two you've given the computer all the instructions it needs. Slowly—very slowly—the *Athena* turns back toward the fuzzy white patch that may be the only link to your own universe.

It takes almost an hour, judging by the *Athena's* chronometer, before you can completely reverse course and start heading for the white patch. You have no idea how far away it is or how fast you're going. Your instruments still indicate that the *Athena* is doing the impossible—traveling at infinite speed—so you have no idea what your speed really is. You should see the white hole growing larger as you get closer. But it doesn't—it continues to get smaller, as if you were still heading away from it!

Nick works on figuring out an explanation. At last he reports. "Our computer is stumped. It's almost useless in this universe!"

"All I can think of," you say, "is that we're in some kind of gaseous green river that's carrying us along with it, away from the white hole, and the current is so strong we can't make any headway against it."

Turn to page 15.

66

You and Nick settle yourselves in for crash position. Your ship is designed to easily withstand a 15-mile-an-hour impact, but will you be able to burrow through the planet's surface, and if so, what will you find inside?

About a mile from the surface, reverse gravity becomes so strong that you're forced to apply full power. It's a strange feeling—diving at full speed toward ground that is trying to fling you back into space!

You watch the altimeter ticking off the distance to the planet's surface. Nick catches your eye.

"This is really a long shot," he says.

"Yeah, I was just thinking that," you say. "It's about as risky as diving into a black hole."

Suddenly the ship hits the ground, jostling you in your seats. A second later the windows are blacked out as you tunnel into the soft, claylike substance. You keep your eyes on the instruments.

"So far, so good," Nick says.

"Reduce power by half," you say. "The repulsion force is declining."

"But the clay is getting denser here," Nick says. "It's slowing us down."

You glance at the data display. The ship is now several hundred yards beneath the surface.

Suddenly the thruster output needles drop to zero.

"We've lost power," Nick cries. "Clay must have seeped into the valves."

Turn to page 54.

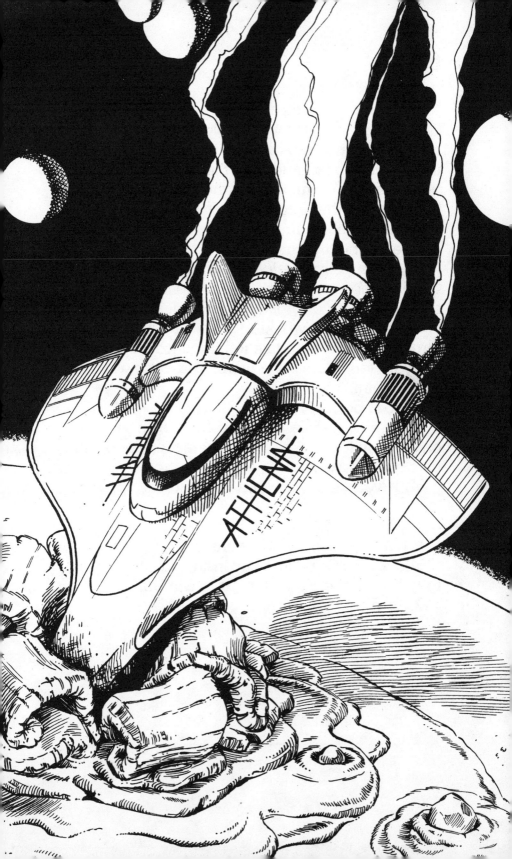

68

"You make the repair, Nick," you say.

He doesn't answer. He simply slips on his gloves and helmet and grabs a tool kit. In a moment he is through the door and into the air lock. It shuts behind him. You make sure the computer countdown is on the frequency of the radio in his helmet. It will be important for him to hear it. You're listening yourself.

Seconds to irreversibility: 48, 47, 46 . . .

A light goes on on the security panel. It shows the outer hatch door is open. Good. That means Nick is outside, working his way toward the thruster. You want to talk to him, encourage him, but you don't dare say a word. You don't want to distract him.

32, 31, 30, 29 . . .

It's terrible just waiting. You can't even see him on the monitor—there's no camera trained on that part of the spacecraft.

You wonder if Nick has reached the thruster joint.

15, 14, 13, 12 . . .

What's happening out there? you wonder.

You feel panic building up inside you. You want to help, but there's nothing you can do.

7, 6, 5 . . .

Time is running out!

Turn to page 85.

Nick is staring at the instruments. "This is incredible. It's as if gravity is working backward—pushing us away!"

"Of course—that's it!" you cry. "That's why we couldn't get back to the white hole—it was repulsing us, pushing us away."

"Oh, no," Nick says. "How can we ever land on a planet here? The moment we turn off the power we'll go catapulting into space."

"There is one possibility," you say. "If by some chance this planet is hollow and we could get inside it, then we could walk around on the inside of the shell—like two ants crawling on the inside of a hollowed-out pumpkin."

"Maybe so," Nick says. "But what makes you think the planet might be hollow? There aren't any hollow planets in *our* universe!"

"That's because of gravity," you say. "But here we're seeing *reverse* gravity that could hollow out the middle of the sphere as all the material there flies up toward the planet's inner surface."

"Maybe," says Nick. "But it sounds farfetched to me. Besides, how could we get to the planet's inner surface? There's no sign of any cracks or holes."

"It looks like a rather soft material to me," you say. "If we hit the surface at full power we might be able to burrow in—this ship is designed to take heavy shocks."

Nick shakes his head. "It sounds like suicide to me."

Turn to page 110.

"I think we should stay where we are," you say to Nick. "It was a miracle that we got here in the first place. I think it would take about ten miracles to get us back through the white hole."

"I feel the same way," Nick says.

"Tell me, Baru—" you start to say, but suddenly the alien is gone! You stand there, stunned.

You and Nick look at each other helplessly. "I don't think we'll see Baru again," you say. "I think Baru decided we didn't need any more help."

"But we need Baru just to help us here on this weird planet," Nick says.

"I don't think so," you say. "Baru said they were making it into a perfect planet. We have been told all we need to survive. It will be just as wonderful as Earth, and we'll live forever and never grow old."

Nick looks at the sky, at the violet-hued ocean, and at the upside-down mountains. "It is a beautiful place," he says, "but will we ever be happy if we never see another human again?"

"I'm not sure," you say. "But we can still have hope. Humans love to explore. Someday, I'll bet, they'll enter the black hole again and find us. And since we will never grow old, we'll be here when they come."

The End

"What do you think of what it's telling us?" Nick asks.

"I think it's pretty clear," you say. "We're in the same galaxy, but not at the same time—we've come out millions of years in the past or millions of years in the future."

As you finish saying this, the computer confirms your guess:

Time is approximately nine million, eight hundred thousand years in the future.

"If that's so," Nick says, "why are the other galaxies still pretty much where they were?"

"If you'll remember how far away they are, then you'll know," you say. "It's as if you were driving along in a car at fifty miles an hour and closed your eyes for a few seconds. When you opened them, nearby trees and houses would be behind you, in a different direction than when you last looked, but a distant mountain would still be in the same direction."

At the same time you're punching instructions into the computer: *Locate earth and sun—set course to intercept them. Give estimated time of arrival.*

Fortunately, the sun and earth are close by— only a few hundred light years away. You and Nick settle down for a long hibernation. When you wake up you'll be home, ten million years after you left. You go to sleep dreaming about what the earth might be like.

The End

"How long were you out there?" Nick asks. "I don't know what hit me."

"Turbulence, perhaps, when we crossed the event horizon," you explain.

Nick looks out. "I don't see any stars."

You shake your head. "We're cut off from the rest of the universe. We've entered the black hole."

Nick looks up at the chronometer. "We must be almost at the . . ."

"Singularity." You complete his thought. "We better get in our restraints."

Nick is still groggy. You apply a sterilizing bandage to his wound and help him back to his station. Then you repressurize the cabin and secure yourself for what is to come.

Turn to page 88.

"They were worried about something," Nick says.

"They're at least eight feet high," you say. "If there are predators around, they must be pretty big."

You and Nick look around cautiously. You see some big, lazy-looking insects flitting around the flowering plants, and a swarm of beautiful butterflies flying past, but otherwise no sign of animal life.

"We've got to find a source of food," Nick says. "Do you think we should take a look at the plants those bird creatures were eating?—they might be all right for us. Or should we look for water first?"

If you decide to inspect the plants,
turn to page 94.

If you decide to look for water, turn to page 36.

A few moments later the reply comes back. The laws of physics no longer apply here. Neither logic nor knowledge will help you decide. Your future will be determined by quantum fluctuations.

Punch in either the number 1 or the number 2.

One of these numbers will produce the correct decision. The answer cannot be determined until you have decided.

Nick is also watching the screen. "Quantum uncertainty. I thought it might come to this. Punch in a number—there's not much time. . . ."

So this is it—you have reached the realm where logic no longer applies. Your fate is strictly a matter of chance.

If you punch number 1, turn to page 60.

If you punch number 2, turn to page 43.

"I don't care what the rules of physics are here," you say. "I agree—I don't think we'll survive by crashing headfirst into a planet."

"Okay," Nick says. "Then let's look around and see what else we can find."

As you're directing the computer to shift course, Nick taps your shoulder. "What's that on number three monitor?"

"It's a comet," you exclaim. "And the objects beyond it look like meteors. They must be debris from our own universe that's fallen into the black hole and come out on this side."

"The odds against anything surviving that journey are a million to one," Nick says. "For everything we see, a million other objects must have been crushed into the singularity."

"That shows how strong that black hole is," you say. "It moves through space like a giant vacuum cleaner. Most things get stuck in the dust bag, but a few get through. We were very lucky."

"Well, at least this gives us hope," Nick says. "We might find a planet like earth, something better to land on than these smooth gray spheres."

"Even if one *were* just like earth," you say, "we'd still have a problem because of reverse gravity in this universe. If we tried to walk around, reverse gravity would pull us up into space."

"We'd have to find caves to live in," Nick says. "Then we could walk around on the ceiling."

Turn to page 35.

"Let's get out of here, Nick," you say.

You activate the reverse thrusters and slowly increase power.

Nothing happens.

"Keep increasing power," Nick says.

"I don't think we should," you say. "We might break loose so fast it would be hard to control the ship."

"Ease power the second we're loose," Nick says.

You keep applying pressure on the rear thrusters. The engines are straining. You can hear their high-pitched whine right through the skin of the ship. Suddenly the ship moves. It reverses rapidly toward the outer surface of the planet.

You quickly ease off the throttles. A split second later there is an explosive sound in the thrusters— something like a hugely amplified cough. You're thrown back in your restraints as the ship brakes to a stop.

Turn to page 115.

You and Nick stand on the inner shell of the gray planet. You're exhausted and covered with the congealed, gray, claylike substance. Your jet packs are useless, and your food supplies are almost gone, but you're alive, and you're breathing pure, oxygen-rich air. The temperature is quite warm, and you shed your mud-caked space suits. You feel a lot more comfortable in the workout suits you wear underneath.

Neither of you is talking. You're trying to make sense out of what you see around you. The ground under your feet is a sort of blue moss. In some places rough gray rock protrudes above the surface. You guess it's made of the same substance as the gooey clay you tunneled through, hardened when exposed to the air. The land around you reminds you somewhat of Earth. There are no trees, but there are giant plants, many of them much taller than you. Some look like enormous tulips and have huge red and yellow flowers that wave in the breeze twenty feet or so in the air. The moss beneath your feet and the stems and leaves of the plants are all a delicate shade of blue. You can't figure out where the light comes from. There's no sun anywhere to be seen, just a soft, clear glow.

Go on to the next page.

80

You crane your neck upward, turning to see in all directions. The sky is most amazing of all, except there really is no sky, or any horizon at all, because the land in the distance—beyond the tall plants and the low hills—curves slowly upward until it arches up over the top of the sky. Directly over your head is a range of rocky mountains that point down at you! Near the highest peaks—where on Earth snow might lie—are patches of green—perhaps green moss.

Another part of the "sky" has an almost clear, amber color and seems perfectly smooth. It could be a desert, or even a sea.

Turn to page 82.

"Let's try to burrow inside this planet," you tell Nick. "I'd rather try something desperate than just drift aimlessly through space until we run out of oxygen."

It's just a hunch of yours that the planet ahead is hollowed out. But the more you think about it, the more your theory makes sense. Almost everything else in this universe seems to be the opposite of what you're used to.

"I'm with you," says Nick, who is already punching instructions into the computer.

You both watch the planet growing larger as the *Athena* races toward it. Its surface looks more and more like clay. Meanwhile, your computer is continually applying more power to maintain speed. It seems clear now that reverse gravity increases as you get closer to an object, the same way regular gravity does in your own universe.

"It might be too strong for us to penetrate even with full power," Nick says.

You do some fast calculations. "I think we can make it all right. We should be able to hit the surface at close to fifteen miles an hour by applying maximum power."

"Let's just hope that gravity doesn't start pulling us down, the way it does in our own universe," Nick says. "We'd be wiped out."

You nod. "That's a chance we have to take—along with a lot of others. One good thing—if we get stuck in the planet's surface, the reverse gravity will help us get out."

Turn to page 66.

82

"It's a beautiful world," Nick says. "And the air is fresh and pure."

"That's lucky," you say, "because I don't think we'll ever be able to leave."

"*Shhh!*" Nick grabs your arm. "Look to the left."

On a sloping plain a few hundred yards away you see a group of very large, yellowish, two-legged creatures. They look rather birdlike, except they are furry, rather than feathered, and have no wings.

"Don't move," you whisper to Nick. "Let's see what they do."

You watch these creatures as they move slowly across the plain, stopping from time to time to feed from some plant growing up from the moss. A few of the larger ones bring up the rear. They seem to be guardians of the others, often stopping to sniff the air and look cautiously around. One of the smaller ones starts to run off to the side. A big one makes a fast, clicking sound. The little one stops short, then bounds back toward the group. You watch, fascinated, as they climb the gentle hill beyond the meadow and disappear over the crest.

Turn to page 74.

84

Nick has already asked the computer what options are available. And now the answer's coming up on the screen.

Option 1: Reverse course at full power; in 13.6 hours you will be sufficiently free of magnetic interference for your radar image to be visible to the observer ship.

Option 2: Maximum power; set course for planet Nicron.

No other options.

"What do you think, Nick? Shall we ask what percentage chance there is on each option?"

He shakes his head. "It won't compute. Too many variables. We don't know where the observer ship—the *Nimrod*—is. It may already be on its way back to base instead of hanging around the fringes of the black hole. As for Nicron—we know it's the nearest planet in the Tau Gamma system."

You glance at the chronometer. You're almost at the event horizon of the black hole—the point beyond which nothing can escape!

If you try to catch up with the Nimrod, *turn to page 41.*

If you try to reach the planet Nicron, turn to page 45.

Then you hear Nick's voice. "Mission accomplished—it was no problem at all."

No problem! That's just like Nick—real cool about everything.

"Good going," you say. "Now get back in here. We still have one little problem up ahead—the biggest black hole in the galaxy!"

You wait anxiously for Nick to reach the hatch and let himself in. You touch a few keys on your computer keyboard. In a moment the screen displays the information you want:

Distance to event horizon: 640,800,000 miles.
Distance to singularity: 2,822,000,000 miles.
Speed: .8 C.

A shudder runs through your body. You can survive inside the event horizon. The singularity is another matter. It is the point at the center of the black hole where all matter may be crushed out of existence.

The numbers on the screen make the black hole sound very far away, but ".8 C" means you're traveling at four-fifths the speed of light!

You didn't realize you were this close to the event horizon—the outer limit of the black hole. Once you pass that point there will be no chance of reversing course, even at full emergency power. At that point gravity is so strong that nothing, not even light itself, can escape its pull. But where is Nick?

Then you hear his voice. "I can't open the hatch. It's jammed!"

"Hold on!"

Turn to page 24.

86

You instruct the computer to head the ship directly into the black hole. There's little chance now of approaching at the course and speed that would get you into the wormhole. You're almost certain to be crushed by tidal forces before you reach the singularity—the point where thousands of stars have been compressed into nothingness. It may also be the point where the rules of physics no longer apply, where there may be a passageway to another universe!

Only a few minutes pass before the blackness opens up before you. It is surrounded by a ghostly purple glow—the light of millions of stars, their strange colors caused by the relativistic effect.

You are now inside the event horizon, past the point of no return, even for light itself. Somewhere ahead of you is the singularity.

You're hoping that by some miracle you'll make it through, as the *Athena* plunges ever deeper into the darkness of the black hole.

Turn to page 100.

88

It begins as a little shuddering of the ship. Not the ordinary kind of turbulence—just a slight quivering. Then this motion stops, and everything is frozen. The chronometer has stopped. You know this because you're staring at it. And you can't stop staring at it. You can't look anywhere else. You can't move a muscle. Not even your eyeballs. You can't blink. You can't breathe either, yet somehow you don't need air. Nick must be in the same situation, though you can't see him—you're facing the other way.

Even stranger is the way you feel—as if you are in a dream, though you know you're awake. Perhaps time has stopped. Perhaps you will be frozen like this forever.

You can't move, but you can *feel,* and you've never felt such hopelessness, such despair. Better to have been crushed in a black hole than to be trapped like this, trapped in time, doomed to sit for eternity, staring at the stopped chronometer.

Turn to page 37.

Sixteen hours have passed since you escaped from the gravitational field of the black hole, and its magnetic interference has diminished to a point where your radar will function. Nick is desperately scanning the area where the *Nimrod* should be. He's still trying when you pick up something on the radio. It's coming from a beamer, a missile containing a radio that beams a recorded message.

The repeating message is digitally encoded, and you quickly instruct the computer to decipher it. Then you tell Nick to look at the monitor—the message is already coming up on the screen.

To Athena *from* Nimrod. *Mayday. Mayday. We're finished. Lost power in our main thrusters. We're being pulled into the black hole. By the time you receive this, if you ever do, we'll be gone. Good luck, mates. Farewell.*

You shed tears when you read this. The *Nimrod* is surely doomed—for there is no possibility of its getting on precisely the right course and speed to get through the black hole.

"We don't have enough fuel or oxygen now to reach home base," Nick says, "or even to go to Nicron."

"I'll ask the computer what our options are," you say.

It seems like forever, but it's really only a few seconds before the answer appears on the monitor.

There are no options.

Turn to page 49.

You blast open the hatch, using enough force to make a little crater in the thick, sticky clay that surrounds the spaceship. You and Nick crawl through the hatch and take turns directing blasts from your jet packs. The heavy, gooey material melts from the heat of your jets, then rapidly congeals, leaving a hole that allows you to crawl a few inches more. Foot by foot, yard by yard, you and Nick take turns crawling and blasting your way through the clay. You find you're using a lot more fuel than you had estimated. You have several feet more to tunnel through when Nick's fuel supply runs out.

Now it's up to you alone. You blast a little more clay and move closer. It can't be much farther now, you think. You blast again and gain a few more inches. Then your jet pack quits. It's out of fuel, just like Nick's.

Things look bleak—there's no way you can dig through this stuff without a blaster. You lie in the tunnel, trying to paw your way for the last few feet. Nick is next to you. There's fear in his voice.

Turn to page 105.

92

You and Nick wander inside the hollow planet for three days and three nights, except, as Nick has suspected, there are no nights. The sky is always clear and amber colored. Whenever you get tired you sleep in the beds of lavender moss.

In your travels you see many strange creatures and many beautiful plants. You find plenty of water in the hollows of the amber vines. It tastes as if it came from a cool, clear spring. And the orange, red, and yellow fruits you eat are as sweet and juicy as anything on Earth.

Occasionally you see one of the spike-toothed bears. They often start toward you, but they are very slow. You can outrun them without even running out of breath. Once you reach the lavender moss, you're safe. For some reason they won't come near it.

You see many other creatures as well, but none of them seems hostile. Except for the bears, all the animals of Baru-Kamm seem to be plant-eaters. As for the countryside, it's the most beautiful you've ever seen.

Turn to page 114.

94

You and Nick reach the meadow where the bird creatures were feeding. You soon find the object of their attention—low, bushy plants, loaded with big, juicy red berries. They're all over the place, and most of them haven't been touched. You're wary of eating poison plants—you would never try a strange berry back on Earth. But there's no other food in sight. You pick one of the berries and sniff it. It seems okay. You touch it with your tongue, then you bite off a piece of it. It's good. In fact it's delicious.

"I think it's okay," you tell Nick.

He tries one and then another. "They're not just okay," he says. "They're great."

"Just eat a couple," you say. "Then wait awhile to make sure we can digest them."

But Nick is popping one after another into his mouth. "Nothing that tastes this good can be bad for you," he says. "I didn't realize how hungry I was!"

You're hungry, too, and you eat another. What luck this is—they're the best-tasting fruit you ever ate.

Turn to page 109.

Your name, along with Nick's, is engraved on a brass plaque over the main entrance to the Space Academy. You will always be remembered as one of the great space explorers, though you'll never be as famous as the lucky few who *were* able to make it successfully through the black hole.

The End

96

This is no time to speculate. You only have a few seconds! You work your way along the EV rail, moving forward, away from the thrusters. In a few moments you reach the starboard window of the control station. You look inside. Nick is slumped in his seat. There's a dark reddish spot in his hair—it's blood! You can see that he's still breathing. He must have been knocked unconscious by some object when the ship passed through the event horizon.

You take a wrench from your tool kit and rap on the cabin window. He stirs a little. You beat out the Mayday signal. You hit the window so hard it would break if it weren't made of space glass.

Nick stirs again. He lifts his head. You keep rapping on the window. He looks around dazedly. He sees you! Slowly he staggers to his feet and motions toward the hatch. *He's going to open it!* Luckily he still has his earphones on. "Nick!" you yell into your microphone. "The outer hatch is blown off. You have to depressurize."

Nick nods. Then all is silent. You relax a little. You know he's depressurizing the cabin slowly—compressing the cabin's air into a container so that all loose objects in the cabin won't be sucked out into space when he opens the hatch.

A few moments later he lets you back inside.

Turn to page 73.

98

"The mind force warned us against crossing this river," you say, "probably for good reason. There's a lot we haven't seen on this side of the river. Let's follow it upstream toward those crimson hills."

"Look!" Nick says, pointing next to you.

Of all the odd things that have happened since you passed through the black hole, none seems stranger than this. It's a human—a person about your age, you'd guess, who looks almost like you! The figure waves and walks toward you.

"This can't be," Nick says.

"We must be cracking up," you say.

"Wh-who are you?" Nick blurts out. The person looks nice enough—with wavy, dark hair and twinkling blue eyes. Yet there's something strange about the way it walks, and about the shape of the face. It looks almost as if it had been molded from plastic.

"Call me Baru," the figure says in a pleasant voice.

"Who are you—did you come from Earth?" Nick asks.

"We look human, but in truth we are not. We are the mind of Baru-Kamm."

"Like the butterflies?" you ask.

Turn to page 116.

100

*Turn to
page 95.*

102

You can feel the buttons on the jet pack because your gloves have sensors at the end of each finger. You key in minimum thrust and activate.

Your jet activates with a little burst, sending you rapidly forward. In a second you've reached the thruster, but you're going too fast to grab hold. Your tether snaps like a piece of thread. You're shooting off into space, falling rapidly away from the *Athena!*

Your computer called for too much power. Suddenly you realize why: you're traveling at nearly the speed of light. The computer wasn't programmed to handle the extreme relativistic effects. *Why didn't the designers think of that?*

You don't have time to wonder—you've got to get back to the ship. Frantically, you punch in a reverse thrust. You're wrenched violently by G forces as your course reverses. This time you won't leave power control to the computer— you'll maneuver the old-fashioned way—gauging the right power and thrust. In half a minute you reach the thruster, just as the crack splits open. You hear a rush of air escaping from the *Athena,* then the beginning of an explosion.

The End

104

While Baru is talking, you're looking straight up toward the white hole. All you can see, though, is the other side of the planet—the upside-down mountains and the violet-hued ocean. Suddenly an idea strikes you. "Baru—is there any way we could journey through that white hole and get back to our own universe?"

"That would be great," Nick says. "I wouldn't want to try to get back the way we came."

Baru nods. "We are in the process of building a perfect planet here on Baru-Kamm. It will be filled with wonderful creatures and plants—a few of them you have already seen. I am sure you would find it a fascinating place to live. You would be able to learn and do things you could never do on Earth, or even in your own universe, and you could live forever and never grow old. We understand why you would want to return home, and we will do our best to help you, but we must warn you first that, though we are far more advanced than earthlings, there are limits to what we can do. We could easily pass through a black hole, as you did to get here, but in this universe there are no black holes—only white holes. To enter a black hole one need only dive into it. White holes are more of a problem. The closer you get, the harder they push you away. And even with engines a million times stronger than anything on Earth, you could not push hard enough to enter a white hole."

Turn to page 32.

"We've got to do something—the pressure of this stuff is squeezing the tunnel behind us!" He shines a light back toward the ship. "The clay starts closing again the moment we open a passageway."

"Like one of those self-sealing tires back on Earth," you say.

"Yeah, and now without any jet pack fuel left, we'll never get back to the ship."

You claw at the wall of clay ahead of you, faster and faster.

"Don't panic. We'll think of something," Nick says.

But you are panicked. There's a sea of clay closing in on the two of you. You keep clawing like a crazed animal. You can't keep it up. Your right arm feels weak. You claw with your left hand, again and again—and suddenly you feel nothing in your fingers. They're free, in the open. You've reached the surface!

Turn to page 79.

106

Never have you ever felt so alone. Not only are you trapped in space, but there aren't even any stars to keep you company. The sky looks totally empty. A space traveler is used to the sight of stars and galaxies, shining far more brightly than they appear on Earth. But you are cut off, not only from other humans and shelter, but from the entire universe!

You crawl into the air lock chamber and try Nick again on the radio. No luck. You rap against the door. He should be able to hear it. You rap again, as loudly as you can, and keep rapping. Then you wait. There's still no response.

What's wrong with him? Is he still alive? you wonder. You try to take stock of the situation.

You are now inside the radius from which no light can escape. No telescope on Earth or in outer space could see you, no matter how powerful it was. You are still millions of miles from the singularity in which all matter is crushed out of existence, but you're falling to that point at almost the speed of light. You'll reach it in less than a minute.

Go on to the next page.

If the rules of physics hold true, you'll have no chance of survival. But some scientists have said that the rules of physics don't apply in a black hole because no law can describe what happens when matter is compressed into a geometrical point.

Theories are one thing, but your chances of survival can't be very good—you're not even inside your spaceship! Yet you've got to do something. Why hasn't Nick heard you? He may need your help. Maybe you should blast the door open. If you do, it will depressurize the cabin, and that could hurt Nick—if he is still alive. You weigh the risks a moment and then make a decision.

If you blast the door open, turn to page 26.

If you decide not to, turn to page 55.

Nick and you are so happy eating berries that you forget about the predators the bird creatures were watching out for. You don't hear them coming until they are almost on top of you. Great, bearlike creatures with enormous jaws and teeth like spikes, they are slow and clumsy—you could have outrun them had you seen them in time.

You enjoyed eating those berries, but not as much as the bear creatures will enjoy eating you.

The End

110

You take a long look out the windows at the endless green space, which seems totally empty except for the smooth gray planets. "Well," you say, "we could just keep cruising along and hope to find something else. But wherever we go, we'll still have the same problem of reverse gravity. And our food and oxygen won't last much longer."

Nick stares out the view port. You know he's straining to see something else, a planet more like earth! Finally he turns around and looks at you. "It's up to you, pal."

If you try to hit the gray planet at full speed, turn to page 81.

If you keep cruising, hoping to find something else, turn to page 76.

Everywhere you look there are stars and nebulae. Training your telescope on the heavens, you can make out fuzzy patches of light. Most of these, when you increase the magnification, have a familiar spiral pattern.

"If we're in another universe, it's a lot like our own," you say to Nick. "What's more, we seem to be in a galaxy quite similar to the Milky Way."

"It's possible," Nick says, "that after passing through the black hole, we came out in our own galaxy."

"This is a problem for the computer," you say. "It should be able to tell us our location."

The computer has to analyze the positions of thousands of stars and other galaxies. Fast as it is, it takes almost ten minutes before its response appears on the screen:

Stars here are in very different positions than they should be, but other galaxies are quite close to the positions they should be.

Nothing else shows on the screen, but an amber light indicates that the computer is working on a more precise analysis.

Turn to page 71.

112

"This is a beautiful place," you say to Nick, "but I don't want to stay here forever. I'm willing to take the chance."

"So am I," he says.

"You are brave," Baru says. "We shall do everything we can to help you succeed. And now, take a last look around, because while you are transformed into another state, you will not be conscious. You will not even be able to dream."

Baru steps forward and shakes hands first with you and then with Nick. Then, it is as if you are sleeping a dreamless sleep.

Turn to page 8.

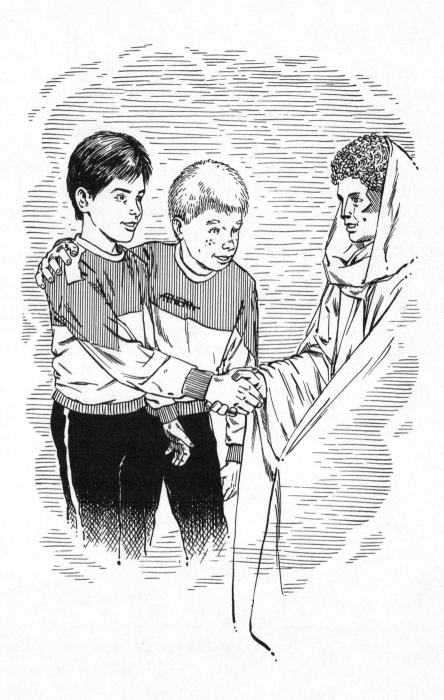

114

After another day's travel you come to a river that blocks your way. It doesn't look too deep or dangerous. The water is exceptionally clear, and you can see that the bottom of the river is made of pink sand. It's not more than twenty yards wide, but the current is running quite fast.

"I guess we have to turn back," Nick says.

"Just a minute," you say. "Maybe we could wade across—we can always turn back if it gets too deep or the current gets too fast."

"I don't know," Nick says. "The mind of Baru-Kamm warned us against it."

"We've got to find someone we can talk to, someone who can help us," you say. "Maybe there's something across the river that the mind of Baru-Kamm doesn't want us to find out—something that could help us."

"Maybe," Nick says. "But do you really think we should chance it?"

If you decide to cross the river,
turn to page 17.

If you decide not to chance it,
turn to page 98.

Nick hunches over the computer, trying to find out what happened.

"Ask for a contamination scan," you say.

Nick punches in some instructions.

In a moment the data appears on the screen:

The reverse thruster valves are jammed. Situation similar to main thruster damage.

"Anything we can do?" Nick asks.

You think a minute, then slowly shake your head. It would be nice to have hope, but you just don't. Your spaceship is hopelessly trapped in the claylike surface of a nameless planet in a nameless universe somewhere beyond the black hole.

The End

116

The figure nods. "But now we have assumed a form like yours so that we can communicate in a friendlier way."

"You said *we*. Are you one person or many?"

"Both," Baru says. "In a way that you could not understand."

"What do you mean when you say you're the mind of Baru-Kamm?" Nick asks.

The figure smiles at the two of you a moment and raises a finger. A lightning bolt flashes across the sky! The mind of Baru-Kamm's hands come together, and thunder rumbles over the valley! Then its hands fall to its sides, and all is still.

Turn to page 40.

ABOUT THE AUTHOR

EDWARD PACKARD is a graduate of Princeton University and Columbia Law School. He developed the unique storytelling approach used in the Choose Your Own Adventure series while thinking up stories for his children, Caroline, Andrea, and Wells.

ABOUT THE ILLUSTRATOR

FRANK BOLLE studied at Pratt Institute. He has worked as an illustrator for many national magazines and now creates and draws cartoons for magazines as well. He has also worked in advertising and children's educational materials and has drawn and collaborated on several newspaper comic strips, including *Annie* and *Winnie Winkle*. He has illustrated many books in the Choose Your Own Adventure series, most recently *The Lost Ninja, Daredevil Park, Kidnapped!, The Terrorist Trap, Ghost Train,* and *Magic Master*. He is also the illustrator of The Young Indiana Jones Chronicles series. A native of Brooklyn Heights, New York, Mr. Bolle now lives and works in Westport, Connecticut.